DEEP DOWN UNDERGROUND

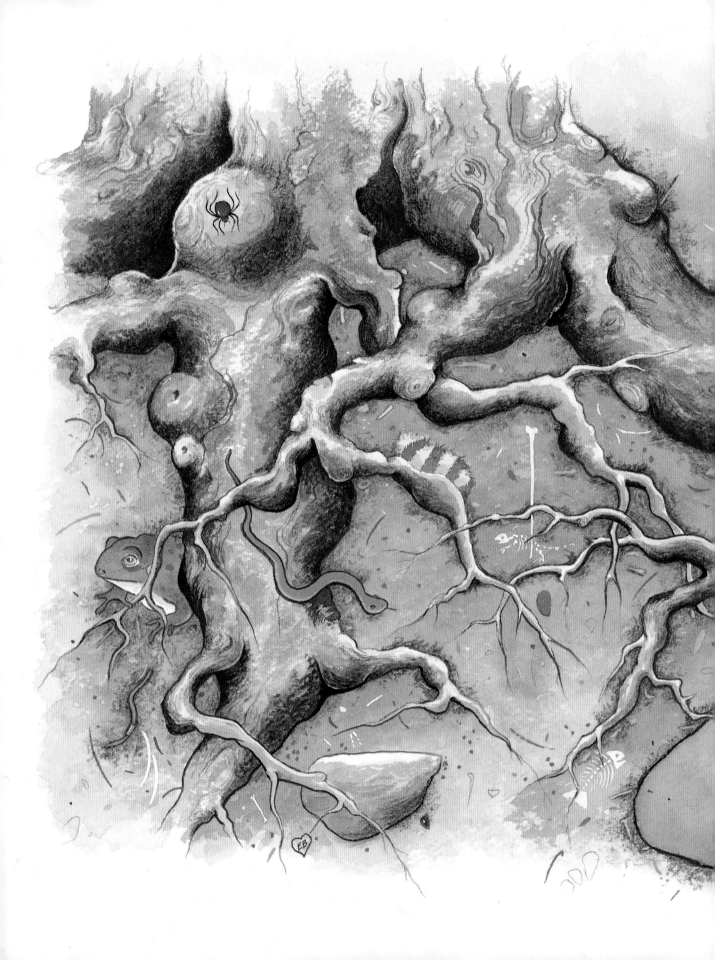

DEEP DOWN UNDERGROUND

by Olivier Dunrea

Macmillan Publishing Company   New York
Collier Macmillan Publishers   London

900311

Printed and bound in Japan First American Edition 10 9 8 7 6 5 4 3 2 1
The text of this book is set in 16 point Caslon Antique. The illustrations are rendered in pen-and-ink and watercolor.
Library of Congress Cataloging-in-Publication Data · Dunrea, Olivier.
Deep down underground / by Olivier Dunrea.—1st American ed. p. cm. Summary: Animals present the numbers from one to ten, as earthworms, toads, ants, and others march and burrow, scurry and scooch deep down underground.
ISBN 0-02-732861-9 [1. Animals—Fiction. 2. Counting.] I. Title. PZ7.D922De 1989 [E]—dc19 88-13534 CIP AC

MOUDIEWORT (pronounced moo-dee-wort)
is a Scottish word for mole.

For Margaret, Nancy, Nick, and Travis,
my Vermont family

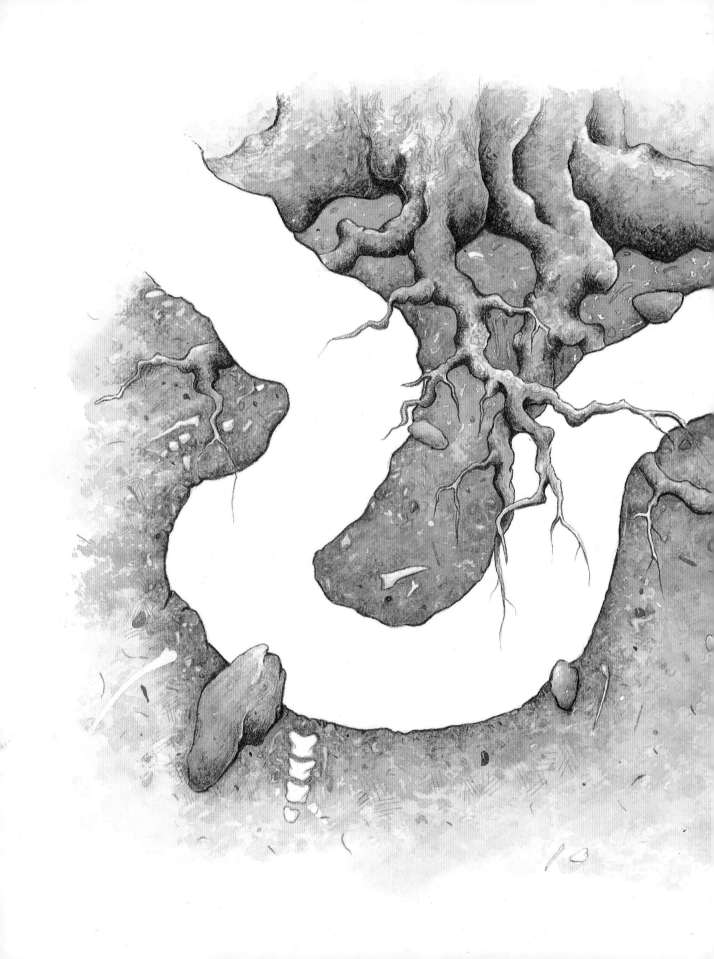

Deep down underground
l wee moudiewort digs and digs
deep down underground.

2 pink earthworms wriggle and wrangle when they hear
1 wee moudiewort digging, digging
    deep down underground.

3 big black beetles scurry and scamper when they hear

2 pink earthworms wriggle and wrangle when they hear

1 wee moudiewort digging, digging
  deep down underground.

4 furry caterpillars scooch and scrunch when they hear
3 big black beetles scurry and scamper when they hear
2 pink earthworms wriggle and wrangle when they hear
1 wee moudiewort digging, digging
   deep down underground.

5 fat spiders dance and prance when they hear
4 furry caterpillars scooch and scrunch when they hear
3 big black beetles scurry and scamper when they hear
2 pink earthworms wriggle and wrangle when they hear
1 wee moudiewort digging, digging
   deep down underground.

6 cold toads burrow and scrape when they hear
5 fat spiders dance and prance when they hear
4 furry caterpillars scooch and scrunch when they hear
3 big black beetles scurry and scamper when they hear
2 pink earthworms wriggle and wrangle when they hear
1 wee moudiewort digging, digging
   deep down underground.

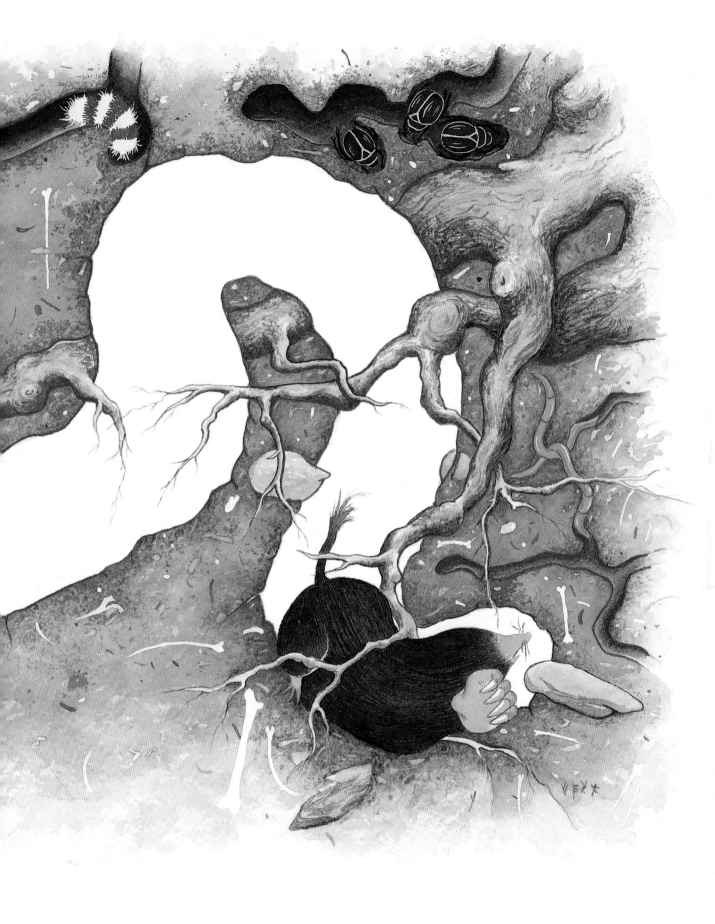

7 gray mice patter and chatter when they hear
6 cold toads burrow and scrape when they hear
5 fat spiders dance and prance when they hear
4 furry caterpillars scooch and scrunch when they hear
3 big black beetles scurry and scamper when they hear
2 pink earthworms wriggle and wrangle when they hear
1 wee moudiewort digging, digging
   deep down underground.

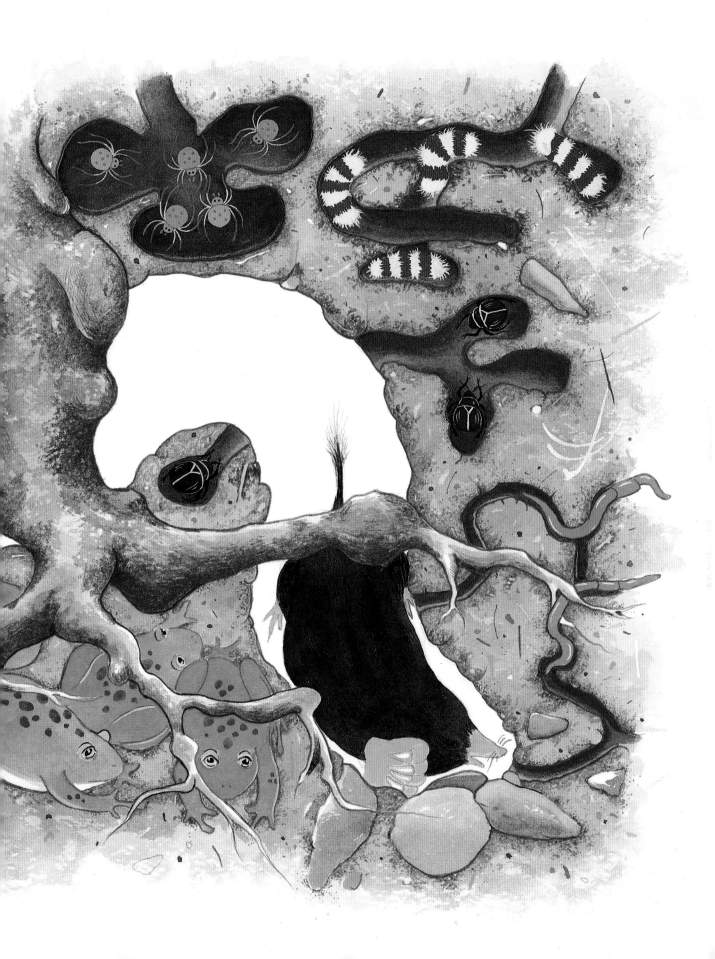

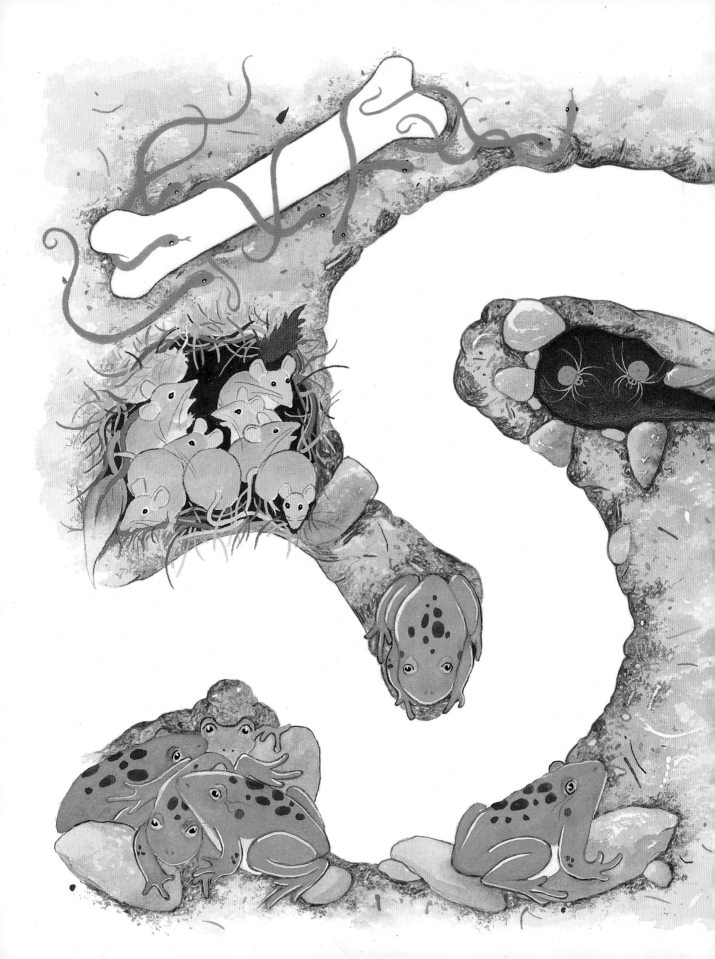

8 green garter snakes slide and glide when they hear
7 gray mice patter and chatter when they hear
6 cold toads burrow and scrape when they hear
5 fat spiders dance and prance when they hear
4 furry caterpillars scooch and scrunch when they hear
3 big black beetles scurry and scamper when they hear
2 pink earthworms wriggle and wrangle when they hear
1 wee moudiewort digging, digging
   deep down underground.

9 armored sow bugs run and roll when they hear
8 green garter snakes slide and glide when they hear
7 gray mice patter and chatter when they hear
6 cold toads burrow and scrape when they hear
5 fat spiders dance and prance when they hear
4 furry caterpillars scooch and scrunch when they hear
3 big black beetles scurry and scamper when they hear
2 pink earthworms wriggle and wrangle when they hear
1 wee moudiewort digging, digging
   deep down underground.

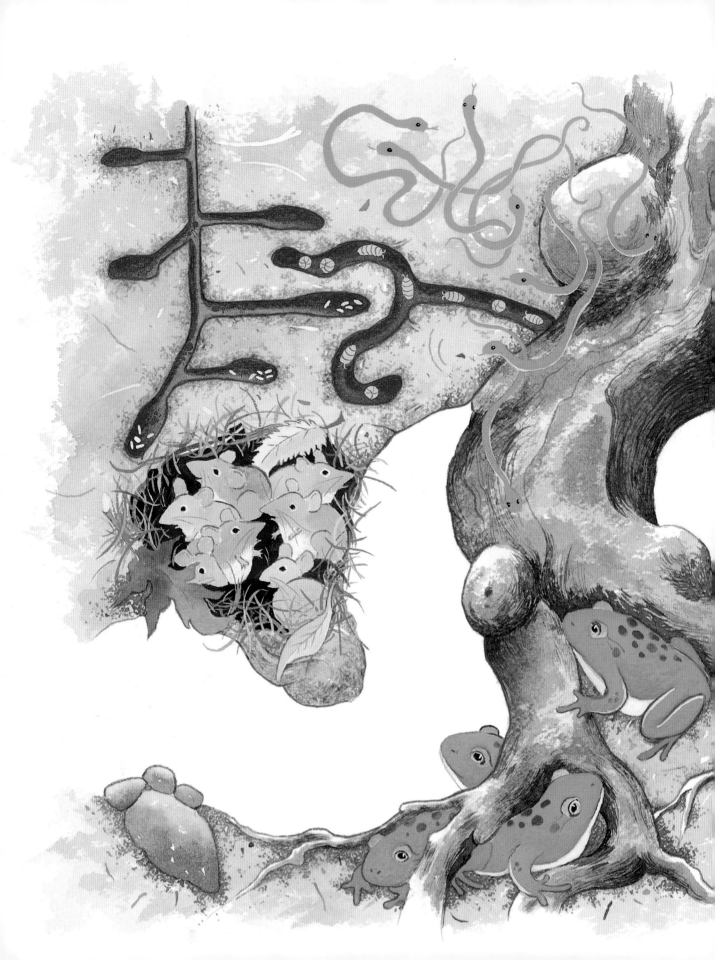

10 red ants march and stamp when they hear

9 armored sow bugs run and roll when they hear

8 green garter snakes slide and glide when they hear

7 gray mice patter and chatter when they hear

6 cold toads burrow and scrape when they hear

5 fat spiders dance and prance when they hear

4 furry caterpillars scooch and scrunch when they hear

3 big black beetles scurry and scamper when they hear

2 pink earthworms wriggle and wrangle when they hear

1 wee moudiewort digging, digging
deep down underground.

Then... 10 red ants STOP marching and stamping when they hear

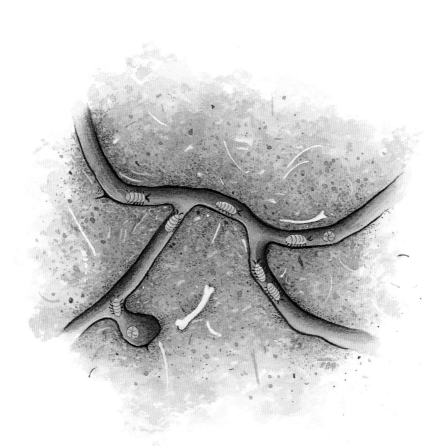

9 armored sow bugs STOP running and rolling when they hear

8 green garter snakes STOP sliding and gliding when they hear

7 gray mice STOP pattering and chattering when they hear

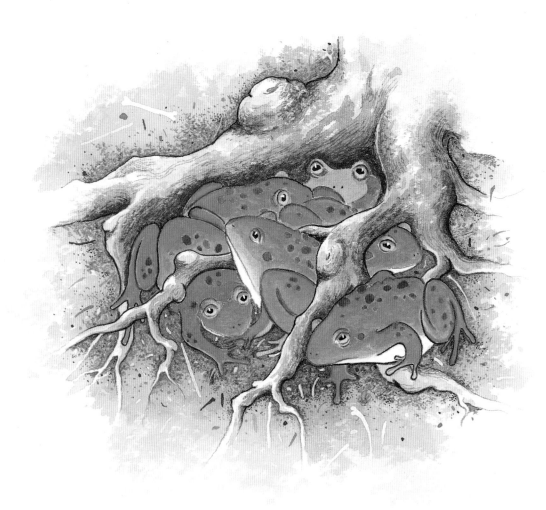

6 cold toads **STOP** burrowing and scraping when they hear

5 fat spiders **STOP** dancing and prancing when they hear

4 furry caterpillars STOP scooching and scrunching when they hear

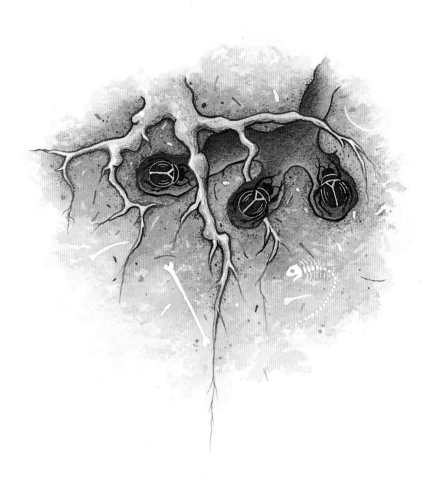

3 big black beetles STOP scurrying and scampering when they hear

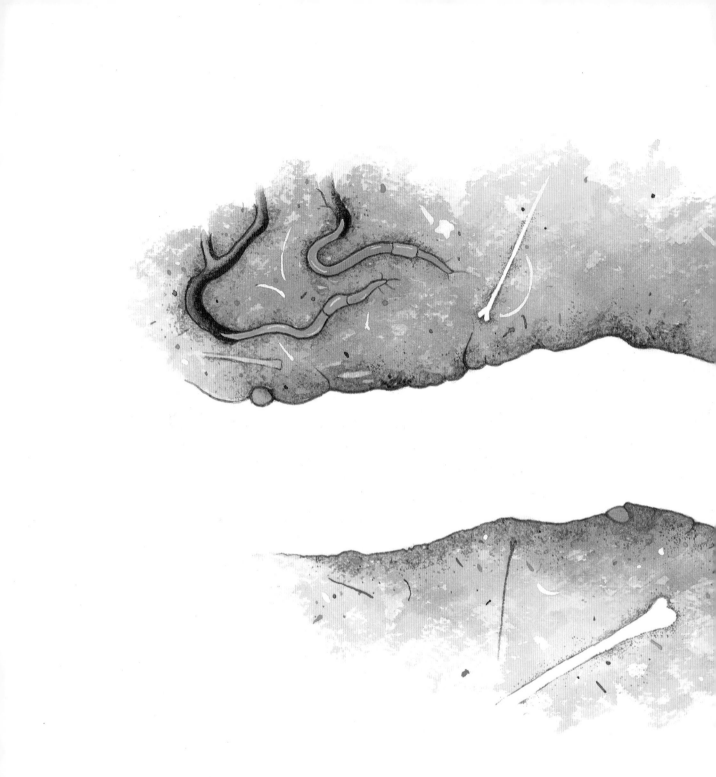

2 pink earthworms STOP wriggling and wrangling when they hear

1 wee moudiewort SNEEZE!
deep down underground.

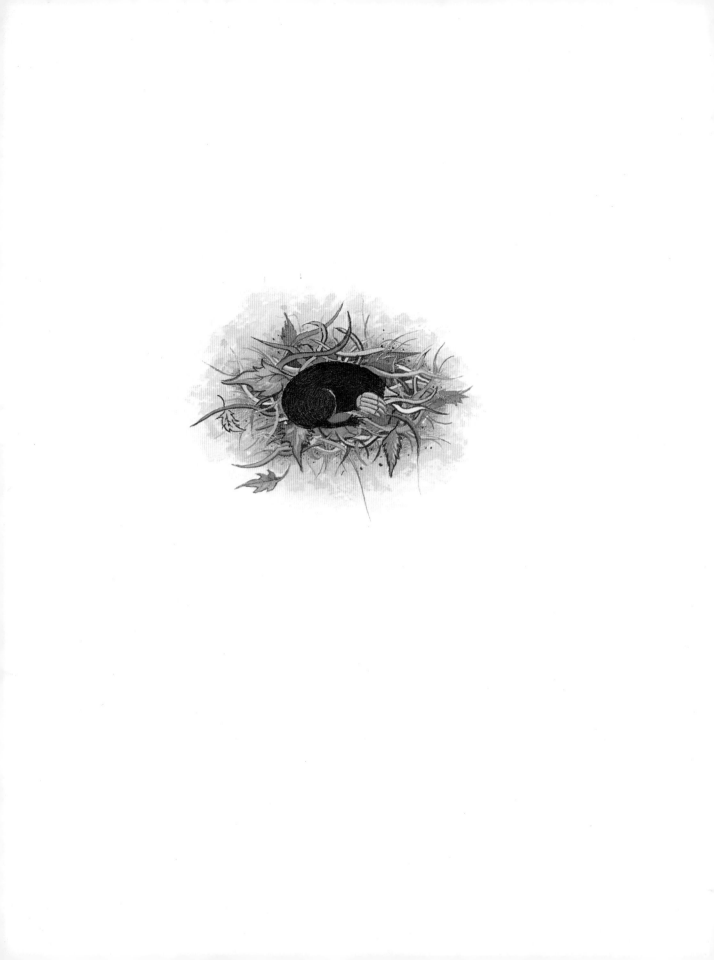